31/

6

THE ANSWERED PRAYER
and Other Yemenite Folktales

◆　◆　◆

Sharlya Gold and
Mishael Maswari Caspi

· THE ·
ANSWERED
PRAYER
and Other Yemenite Folktales

◆

illustrated by Marjory Wunsch

The Jewish Publication Society

PHILADELPHIA · NEW YORK · 5750–1990

Library of Congress Cataloging-in-Publication Data

Gold, Sharlya.
    The answered prayer, and other Yemenite folktales/Sharlya Gold
and Mishael Maswari Caspi; illustrated by Marjory Wunsch.
        p.   cm.
    Summary: A collection of traditional tales from the Jewish
communities in Yemen.
    ISBN 0-8276-0354-1
    1. Tales—Yemen.   2. Legends. Jewish.   [1. Folklore—Yemen.
2. Folklore, Jewish.]   I. Caspi, Mishael. 1932—   .   II. Wunsch,
Marjory, ill.   III. Title.
    PZ8.1.G58An   1990   90-32298
    398.2′095332—dc20   CIP
                                                 AC

10 9 8 7 6 5 4 3 2 1

To all the Isenbergs—the native-born
and the married-ins.   —S.G.

◆

For Nahum.   —M.M.C.

◆

To the memory of Harry Markel.   —M.W.

CONTENTS

◆ ◆ ◆

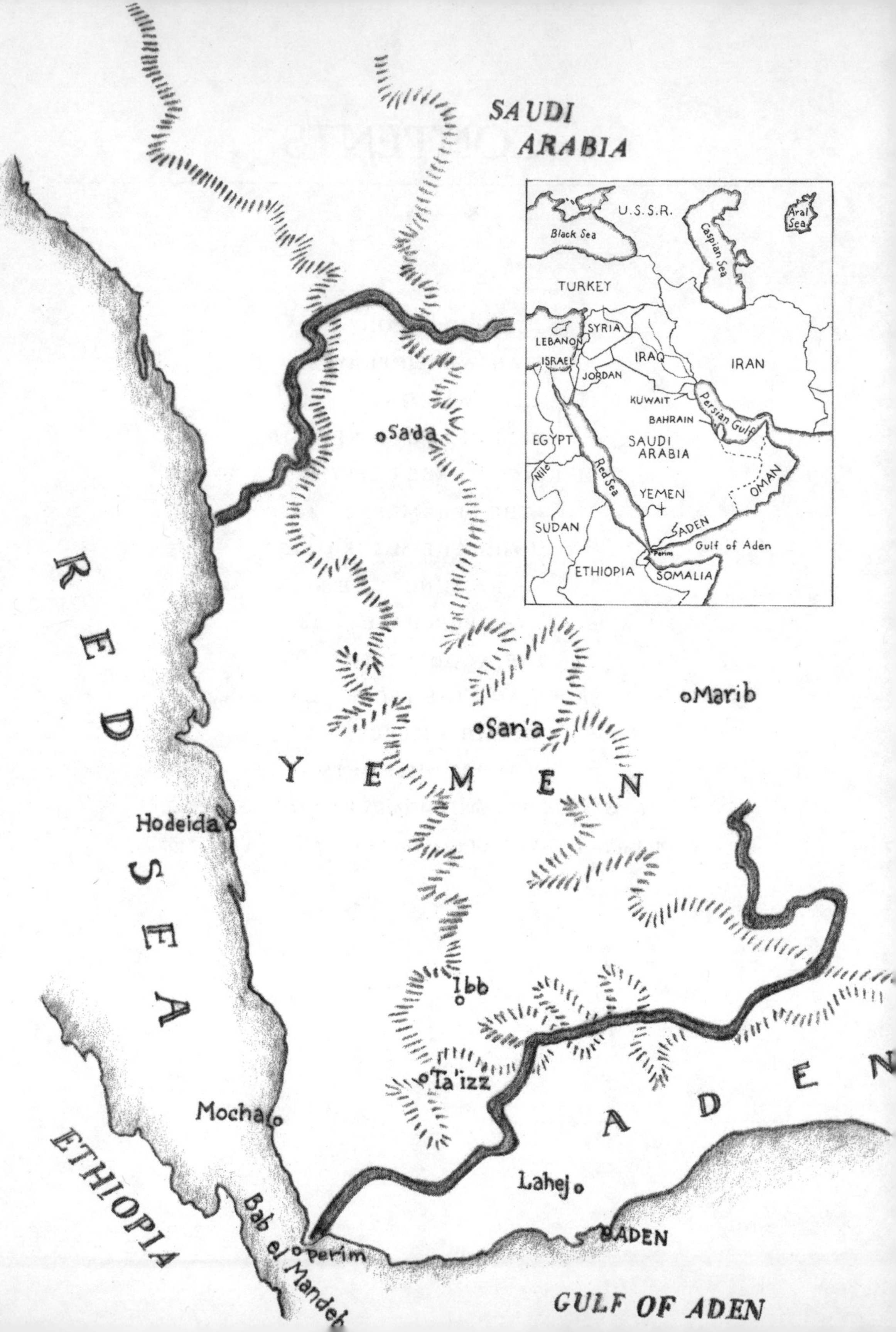
SAUDI ARABIA
U.S.S.R.
Aral Sea
Black Sea
Caspian Sea
TURKEY
SYRIA
LEBANON
ISRAEL
IRAQ
IRAN
JORDAN
KUWAIT
BAHRAIN
Persian Gulf
EGYPT
SAUDI ARABIA
Nile
Red Sea
YEMEN
OMAN
SUDAN
ADEN
Perim
Gulf of Aden
ETHIOPIA
SOMALIA
Sa'da
Marib
San'a
YEMEN
RED SEA
Hodeida
Ibb
Ta'izz
Mocha
ADEN
ETHIOPIA
Lahej
Bab el Mandeb
Perim
ADEN
GULF OF ADEN

INTRODUCTION

◆ ◆ ◆

The Jews of Yemen who devised these tales and passed them from one generation to another did not know "next year in Jerusalem" would be a reality for their descendants. Those early Jews left Babylonia and trekked across the desert sands to the southwestern part of the Arabian Peninsula. They settled in Yemen with the belief that there they could worship in peace and follow God's laws as they saw fit.

They dwelt in harmony with their Arab neighbors, until Yemen became an international battleground. It was fought over and occupied at various times by Abyssinia, Persia, Egypt, Turkey, and Great Britain. The oppressive laws of each conqueror caused great suffering to the Jews, who were also subjected to the whims and impulsive dictates of the local imams and Arab kings.

In the seventh century, Muhammad, a merchant, began a new religion called Islam, which spread throughout all the desert lands of Arabia. Its followers were Muslims, and they tried to convert everyone to the new faith either peaceably or by force.

The Jews, who had their own religion and ancient traditions, refused to accept the ideas of Muhammad. For this defiance they endured additional persecutions. In Yemen, they were deprived of citizenship, and except for barbering and metalworking, most occupations were closed to them. Many became potters, jewelry makers, or sellers of charcoal and wood. The Jews received the lowest-paying jobs and lived in unremitting poverty. Social humiliation was common, too, as Jews were forbidden to ride a horse, wear new clothes, or own a weapon—even for the purpose of self-defense. At times, Jews were forced to surrender their homes to their Muslim neighbors and move into the desert, beyond the protection of a city's walls.

Throughout the centuries, the Jewish communities in Yemen were separated by geography and hostile laws that prohibited them from traveling freely within the country or beyond its borders. But this isolation failed to instill a sense of abandonment and despair. Instead, it strengthened the bonds among Jews within their individual communities.

It also bound them more closely to the Torah, which gave them guidelines for conducting their everyday lives. The Torah taught them how to educate their children, settle quarrels, carry out business transactions, and develop rituals for the important life cycles of birth, marriage, and death. The Torah reassured the Jews of Yemen, as it did Jews all over the world, that one day their suffering would end and they would be taken to the Holy Land, the land of milk and honey. This promise of comfort and hope gave the Yemenite Jews a sense of history and destiny and linked them to the entire Jewish nation.

In 1949 and 1950, that sense of destiny increased when Operation Magic Carpet transported forty thousand Jews, nearly the entire Jewish population of Yemen, to Israel. Following the creation of the State of Israel in 1948, life had worsened for Jews in Yemen and other Arab lands. The Jewish Agency sponsored their rescue in planes owned by Alaskan Airlines and piloted by Americans. Those Jews knew practically nothing of the world outside Yemen. Carrying with them little more than their Torah scrolls and other holy books, they entered the Promised Land.

Dr. Mishael Caspi, a Yemenite Jew born in Israel and fluent in Arabic and Aramaic, took his tape recorder and sought out the new arrivals. He was afraid the Yemenite tales would eventually be forgotten or abandoned as the storytellers took on the ways of their adopted country.

Fortunately, the storytellers needed little coaxing to tell their stories since humor, affection, and advice were part of the collective wisdom they routinely passed from one generation to another. Men were the storytellers in the Yemenite culture, so it is only natural that most of their stories concerned the deeds and preoccupations of men. Women, though, expressed themselves more creatively in songs and poetry rich with wit, wisdom, and romance.

In retelling these stories, we have tried to communicate the spirit of the storytellers as well as our sense of their words. Whether the tales are of an innocent woodcutter who is unjustly accused or of a discontented wife who runs away from her patient husband, they may illuminate our own culture and link us to a past we cannot experience in another way. At the very least, they offer us a glimpse into the beliefs, customs, and practices of Jews who lived every day of their lives by the precepts of the Torah.

THE ANSWERED PRAYER

◆　◆　◆

One cold and rainy day a poor Jew named Salim trudged toward his village, which lay on the other side of the steep mountain in front of him. He had already traveled many miles and was very tired. As he slowly made his way up the steep and muddy road he prayed, "Dear God, I scarcely have the strength to put one foot in front of the next. Please send a donkey to carry me, or else I shall be an old man before I see my home again."

On the road just ahead, two Turkish soldiers were arguing with a Muslim. Salim tried to pass, but one of the soldiers called out to him, "Hey, Jew! Why are you mumbling?"

"I am only praying," protested Salim, but the soldier did not believe him. Grabbing Salim by his *zunner*, the yellow turban all Jews were compelled to wear, he growled, "I should cut your ears off for lying, but as I have a tender heart, I will allow you to carry my donkey to the top of this mountain instead."

Since Salim treasured his ears, cold and wet as they were, he had to obey. He gathered the donkey in his arms and struggled up the mountain. Each step required greater effort than the one before, but he dared not complain. To himself he said, "Salim, you have no luck. You prayed for a donkey to carry you, and now you are carrying a donkey."

When Salim finally reached the top of the mountain and set the donkey down, the soldier said, "Now you should pray, Jew, and give thanks that your big ears still stick out from under your turban."

Wearily Salim went down the other side of the mountain. He did not say a prayer of thanksgiving. In fact, he had no wish ever to pray again. Step by step he plodded on. How good it would be to rest, he thought.

Suddenly Salim heard the sound of hooves and saw a band of Muslim tribesmen galloping toward him. He knew he could not move fast enough to get out of their way and hoped they would ride around him, just as the waters of the Red Sea had parted when Moses held up his hand and rod.

But nothing of the kind happened. A powerfully built rider jerked Salim off his feet, and without even slowing down set him on the horse. The soldier carried him a few miles and dropped him in front of a tent woven of black goat hair. Pride rang in the man's voice. "Here, my lord, is a Jew, as you requested."

Trembling with fear and exhaustion, Salim looked up and met the deep-set eyes of a desert prince. "How . . . how may I serve you, my lord?" stammered Salim.

"My daughter is about to give birth. She is suffering great pain, and you alone can help her."

"Me, my lord?" Salim replied, quaking with fear. "I am not a doctor."

"But you are a Jew, and Jews are a holy people. I know God will listen to you." The prince took a step toward Salim and rested his hand on the hilt of his *jambiyya*, the razor-sharp knife at his side. "Ask God to stop my daughter's pain and give her an easy birth."

Salim wished he were dead, as he well might be in a few minutes. He thought, "With my luck at praying, the princess is surely doomed, and so is her child."

At last Salim said, "I shall do as you wish, my prince, but such an important prayer can only be made from the back of your fastest donkey." Salim really preferred the prince's fastest horse, but Yemenite Jews were forbidden by law to ride horses.

The prince looked puzzled but ordered a donkey to be brought at once. He could hear the moans of his daughter and knew there was no time to lose. Salim lost no time himself in leaping upon the animal's back. In a loud and trembling voice he prayed, "Most merciful God! Please heed my prayer as you have never heeded it before. Send to the prince's daughter terrible, terrible pain! May the birth of her child be more difficult than the birth of a camel!"

The prince let out a roar of anger. How dare the Jew place such a curse upon his daughter and call it a prayer? But before he could open his mouth again to order the Jew's death, Salim clapped his heels against the donkey's rough sides and raced away. At the same moment, word came to the prince that his daughter's pain had stopped. She had given birth to a strong, healthy son.

"All praise to Allah!" shouted the prince. Then he sent his tribesmen in pursuit of Salim.

The swift horses quickly overtook the donkey, and before the dust in the road could settle, Salim once again stood before the prince, who now seethed with anger. Salim trembled in fear. At any moment he expected to hear the *jambiyya* whistle through the air and slice off his head.

The prince said harshly, "I asked you for a prayer, not a curse!"

Salim begged for a chance to explain. Quickly he related what had happened to his prayer for a donkey. His voice quivered as he added, "My prince, try to understand. To save the lives of your daughter and her child, I had to pray for the opposite of what I wanted."

"But why did you pray from the back of my donkey?" the prince wanted to know.

"So that I could save my own life. I knew when you heard my prayer, you would kill me first and ask questions later!"

All at once the prince began to laugh. What a crazy Jew. Now that his daughter was restored to him, he did not care if Salim's prayers were upside down or inside out. "Go in peace, and take the donkey as your reward," he said.

Greatly relieved, Salim thanked the prince and started for home once again. He still had a long way to go, but now he did not care so much. It was only as Salim entered his village did he realize that God, after all, had taken pity on him. God had granted his first prayer and sent him a donkey.

THE WANDERER

◆　◆　◆

Awad lived in a small village in Yemen. He was dissatisfied with his life. Every day he saw the sameness of the village, with crumbling houses, dusty streets, and bony goats nibbling the dry grass. Even the buying and selling, stealing and lying that went on in the *suq* didn't change.

Finally Awad decided to leave his home and wander through Yemen until he came to a place that offered a better life. That is where he would live.

For a long time, Awad followed paths that curved around the barren Yemenite hills. He hiked through rocky valleys and crossed wadis that had not held water for years. He was searching for something he had never seen before, something completely new.

Then one day Awad came to a mountain. He decided to climb it since that was the best way to find out what lay on the other side.

Awad began to climb. After many, many hours of ceaseless struggle, he reached the top. But there on the very top of the mountain stood a wall so high, Awad could not see over it. Tired though he was, Awad's curiosity would not let him rest.

What could be on the other side of the wall? he kept wondering. Walls were built to keep something in or somebody out. At last he drew upon his remaining strength, climbed the wall, and dropped down on the other side. Awad was so exhausted, he fell asleep at once. He barely noticed he was in a village.

In the morning Awad walked along every street. Little notice was taken of him, for his dark hair and beard made him look much like the other villagers. And to Awad the village looked much like the place he had lived all his life. He seemed to recognize the houses, the thick dust of the roads, and the bony goats chewing the dry grass. Even the men in their simple *sirwals* looked like the men of his village.

The wall, of course, made all the difference, for Awad's village had no wall at all. Neither did it have two sturdy gates like those that hung on the wall opposite each other. All that first day Awad watched in amazement as a crowd of people struggled to push open one of the gates. Again and again men threw themselves against the rusty iron plates and shouted at its dust-coated hinges, "Move! Move!"

Each day he saw a small group of people pushing and yelling at the gate. Following the five Muslim times of prayer—dawn, noon, midafternoon, sunset, and dusk—others came to help. At last Awad said to a man who had paused to wipe the sweat from his face with a corner of his *kiffiyeh,* "Tell me, please, just why do you wish to open the gate?"

"Because we recall the stories of our ancestors." The man's black eyes lost their weariness as he went on, "They told us the valley below is green with natural springs of delicious water. Trees, flowers, and grains of every kind grow there, and no one will ever have to go hungry or thirsty again."

Awad felt his heart leap with excitement. To live in that valley would be like living in paradise with the Prophet! Awad decided to remain in the village until the gate was finally opened. Then, like the others, he would settle in the valley.

Awad took the most menial jobs, the ones usually done by the least respected. He carried water, collected goat dung, and helped anyone

who could pay him with food or lodging. Still, no matter where in the village he went, he took care to pass by the gate and listen to those who struggled with it.

One day as Awad was on an errand for the sandalmaker, he heard the gate creak and groan. It was beginning to give way! Awad crowded in among the others and jumped into the air again and again to catch the first glimpse of the fertile valley.

Slowly, slowly the gate moved forward as the people pushed against it with all their strength. But as it swung wide, Awad heard a great commotion behind him. He turned about and saw the other gate burst open, too. An enormous crowd of people was pushing their way through it and crowding into the main street of the village.

Awad stared at the newcomers. Their bearded faces were eager with hope and longing. The dust of years clung to their *sirwals* and sandals. The grime lay along the flanks of their skinny goats, from whose mouths grass hung like limp, brown whiskers.

"Who are you, and what do you want?" cried out the man who had once spoken to Awad.

Their leader answered, "We are from the valley below, and we want to settle here. Long ago our ancestors told us within this wall was a beautiful land. They said it would provide us with everything we should ever need."

On hearing these words, Awad lost all desire to settle in the valley. Instead he walked out through one of the gates and returned to his own home.

In the years ahead, whenever Awad felt the need to travel to an unknown place, he took a walk about his own village. It was as new—and as familiar—as any place he had ever seen.

OVEDIAH'S FORTUNE

◆ ◆ ◆

Once in San'a there lived a poor Jew named Ovediah who envied the rich merchants with their bulging leather purses. He yearned with all his heart to be rich, too.

Ovediah made a small living by doing odd jobs. He worked hard and long, yet at the end of each day he never had more than a single rial to show for his efforts. As time passed, Ovediah became obsessed by the notion that if he could acquire just one additional rial, his luck would change and he would become a rich man. So he worked even harder. He rose before dawn and went to bed long after the stars appeared in the dark Yemen sky. He even scrimped on the small amount of food he ate. But it made no difference. Ovediah always ended the day with only a single rial.

Once a customer paid him too much. Instead of pointing out the mistake, Ovediah quietly rejoiced. Today he would possess another rial! But a moment later the customer returned demanding his money back and threatening to turn Ovediah over to the court.

Another time Ovediah actually found a rial. It was wrapped in a piece of brightly colored cloth and lay near a well-traveled path that led to the *suq*, the Muslim marketplace. Ovediah hid the cloth in his shirt. Now he had two rials!

Then he saw a boy coming slowly toward him. He seemed to be

searching for something. As he neared Ovediah, the boy raised his dark, tear-filled eyes. "Have you seen my money?" he asked. "My master wrapped it in a cloth and sent me to the *suq* to buy *qat* for him. He will beat me when he learns I have lost it."

"What a pity," Ovediah said, touching his shirt to assure himself the cloth was still there. But just at that moment he stumbled against a loose stone in the road. Ovediah cried out and seized his injured foot. As he hopped about in pain, the cloth fell from his shirt and dropped to the road.

Like a flash the boy fell upon it. Turning on Ovediah, he charged, "You are a thief!"

"Coins have no names on them," Ovediah retorted, but he again had only one rial.

Yehiel the water carrier sometimes chided Ovediah about his preoccupation with money. "Face it, Ovediah," he would say. "You can change nothing. Whatever is . . . is."

Ovediah would not listen. He doubled his efforts, but he couldn't succeed in doubling his earnings.

One evening after havdalah, the evening service separating the end of the Sabbath from the beginning of the new week, Yehi-el said to Ovediah, "Last week a merchant told me there is such a shortage of glass shades here in San'a that they cost one rial each."

"What has that to do with me?" Ovediah replied.

"In Hodeida, five glass shades can be purchased for one rial," said his friend with a sly grin.

Ovediah needed no more than one hand to count the profit he would make if he bought shades in Hodeida and sold them in San'a! At last his luck was changing.

Too excited to sleep, Ovediah waited impatiently for the first light of morning and the opening of the *bab-alroom*, the city gate. He didn't even take time to eat. "When I am rich, I shall dine like a king," he promised himself.

The journey took almost three days, and by the time Ovediah reached Hodeida, a port city on the Red Sea, he was so hungry and thirsty and weary, he could scarcely stand. But after he purchased the glass shades, such great plans filled his head that he forgot his discomfort. When he came again to Hodeida, he would buy twenty-five shades to sell in San'a and the next time one hundred and twenty-five! He would buy a donkey and call himself Ovediah the lamp shade merchant.

Charged with new energy, Ovediah immediately set off for Sanca. His hunger and thirst clamored for attention, but he pressed on. He was determined to reach Sanca as quickly as possible.

At the end of the second day, darkness overtook Ovediah before he could reach Sanca. He knew the *bab-alroom* would be locked until morning. Rather than sit outside the city wall all night, Ovediah decided to find someplace to sleep.

A little farther down the road, he stopped at the house of a farmer, who gave him permission to sleep with the goats. The generous man also gave Ovediah a piece of goat's cheese and a dry pita to eat.

Ovediah carefully set the treasured lamp shades near him. He stretched out on a pile of straw and thought with contentment about the fortune that would soon be his.

He soon fell asleep and began to dream. He found himself in the Tihama, a hot and humid place. His throat ached from thirst. Perhaps it was from the salty goat's cheese he had eaten or from the dust he had swallowed during his long journey. In his dream he began to search desperately for something to drink.

Suddenly Ovediah saw himself on the bank of a mighty river. Droplets of water sprayed into the air as the river raced by, but they were beyond Ovediah's reach. The swift current frightened Ovediah.

"It might sweep me away if I try to get a drink," he said to himself. He decided to follow the river until it became more gentle.

Impatiently Ovediah bent his steps to the river's course and came at last to its headwaters, which poured from a huge crevice in a mountain. Eagerly Ovediah stretched his hands to the silvery spray that shot out from the sides. But before he could catch a single drop a tall man dressed in a white *kiffiyeh* stopped him and explained, "This is not an ordinary river. It is the fortune of all people, and no one may interfere with it in any way."

Ovediah became so excited, he forgot all about his aching throat. Since the river was the fortune of all people, then it must contain his fortune, too. Ovediah begged to learn what the future held for him.

The guard would give no hint. "No one may know the future until it becomes the present. Go away."

But Ovediah stubbornly refused to leave until at last the guard gave in. He led Ovediah to another face of the mountain and pointed to a tiny crack. "There. That is your fortune," he said.

Ovediah watched as a single drop of water fell from the crack. A second drop fell. Then nothing.

Ovediah became desperate to widen the crack. In his dream he kicked wildly at the mountain and hurt his foot. But he did not stop. Again and again he kicked at the crack.

Suddenly the pain in his foot became so intense that Ovediah awoke. He blinked in confusion and looked about for the river and the guard, but he was alone. The steamy straw still smelled of goats, and his mouth felt drier than ever. Then Ovediah looked down at his aching foot and saw that he had kicked over the package containing the glass shades. All of them were broken—except one.

He could sell it in San'a. For one rial.

THE KING'S THREE
QUESTIONS

◆ ◆ ◆

Hard times had come upon the Jews who lived in San'a, the capital city of Yemen. Their Muslim neighbors murmured against them. One said he had overheard a group of Jews plotting against the king. Another vowed he heard the Jews praying for a drought to ruin the millet crop. Still another insisted he had seen the building plans for a new Jewish house. It would be taller than any Muslim dwelling, and that was clearly against the law.

The Jews protested their innocence, but many were arrested. Some were wounded. A few were killed. Rabbi Salih, the leader of the San'a Jews, visited one home after another. He tried to comfort the injured and the families of the dead.

Then, as if the Jews did not have enough trouble, the king issued a decree. It said that before Ramadan, the Islamic holy month of fasting, all Jews must leave San'a. The Muslim population was growing larger, the king explained, and the Jews' houses were needed by his own people.

Life was hard enough for Jews in San'a, but outside the city walls it would be much worse. Bandits often preyed on small villages and settlements. They stole whatever they could and sometimes even carried off people to make them slaves.

Rabbi Salih went to plead with the king. "Most gracious king, I beg of you to annul your decree. Muslim law forbids Jews to carry weapons, even to defend ourselves. If we are forced to live beyond the protective walls of San'a, we shall surely be killed or captured and sold into slavery."

"I am a fair man," the king replied. "Bring me a Jew who will correctly answer the three questions I put to him, and I will do as you ask. But if he fails, the Jews will have to leave San'a at once."

With a heavy heart Rabbi Salih returned to the Jewish community. He had heard of Christian and Muslim kings who used this question-and-answer ploy to justify cruel laws against the Jews. The questions were often so unfair they could not be answered.

He gathered everyone together in the synagogue and said to them, "The king has promised to annul his decree if I can bring someone to answer three questions. If the answers are wrong, we shall have to leave San'a immediately."

The rabbi waited for someone to volunteer, but no one considered himself wise enough to answer the king's questions. The Jews of San'a knew a great deal about Torah and Talmud but little of the world in which the king lived.

At last someone asked Rabbi Salih, "Why don't you answer the questions yourself? You are the wisest of us all."

Rabbi Salih pulled at his white beard. "As the king asked me to bring someone, it is obvious he did not want to put his questions to me."

At last Sa'id, a dark-haired, ten-year-old boy, said, "I will go. My mind is not yet clouded by much study. I place all my trust in God."

Since the rabbi had no one else, he agreed to send the boy. Possibly Sa'id's innocence would soften the king's heart.

When the king saw the slender, simply dressed boy, his royal face darkened with anger. The chief adviser raged. "How dare the Jews send a child to answer your questions?"

But then the king looked into the brown eyes of the boy. They were untroubled and without fear. Perhaps the child was more than he seemed. Perhaps he was a scholar beyond his years.

Respectfully Sa'id asked for the first question, but the king put him off. "Let us first have breakfast together," he said.

Sa'id and the king ate from the same dish with their fingers, as was the custom. They talked together, and the king learned Sa'id was very poor. He lived with his mother and uncle in the Jewish quarter of the city.

The boy asked again for the first question, but the king delayed once more. "Let us have lunch together. Then we shall stroll about my palace."

The afternoon passed pleasantly. Sa'id told the king he had only one garment, the one he was wearing. He hoped one day to become a merchant in the *suq*, the marketplace. Then he asked once more for the first question.

"You shall have it," answered the king. He pretended to think deeply and then said, "How many stars are in the sky?"

The boy thought to himself of God's promise—that the Jews themselves should be as numerous as the stars of the sky and the sands of the earth. But he did not speak of these thoughts. He simply answered with a very large number and added, "Am I not correct, my king? Or have you counted the stars more recently than I?"

The king, of course, had never counted the stars and was unable to prove the boy wrong. When the chief adviser acknowledged that Sa'id had given a suitable answer, the king tried to hide his annoyance. He bade the boy good evening and returned to his palace. He would ask the second question in the morning.

Sa'id slept well. On the next day the king said to him, "Come, let me show you my garden."

Many pomegranate and orange trees grew in the garden. There were flowers and fountains. The hours passed easily as Sa'id and the king strolled about. The king waited until he felt sure the boy was overwhelmed by the beauty and fragrance of the place. Then he said quickly, "The second question: How much water do I have in my garden?"

Sa'id replied, "My king, walk with me to the creek and stir it with your hand. Then I will answer your question."

The creek that flowed nearby seemed to be made of moonlight. The king slipped his hand into the gentle current and let it caress his fingers. When he withdrew his hand, Sa'id asked, "How many drops of water remain on your skin?"

"That is impossible to know," the king protested.

"Yet, beloved king, you wish me to know how much water is in your entire garden. Is that not impossible, too?" replied Sa'id.

The chief adviser whispered to the king. The boy's answer was suitable.

Again the king tried to conceal his displeasure. He bade Sa'id a good night, saying, "Tomorrow, I shall ask the last question. If you answer well, you may have whatever is in my power to give. If you answer poorly or not at all, you and your people must leave San'a before nightfall."

The next day the king placed three apples on a table and said, "Count the apples and tell me the number."

Rabbi Salih, who had accompanied Sa'id for the third question, groaned to himself. The question seemed so simple, yet it was the hardest of all. Would the boy see through its trickery?

Sa'id answered easily, "There is only one, my king."

The king laughed. "Now I have you. As I suspected, you cannot count."

The boy looked surprised. "Did you think I would count the apples as a Christian might count them: one, two, three as in the Trinity?"

He shook his dark head. "I count as the Muslims and the Jews count. The word *one* means One God. After saying *one*, I cannot say *two* and *three* because they suggest more gods. Muslims and Jews agree there are no other gods. Is that not true, my king?"

The king did not need his adviser's opinion this time. The boy had answered very well. "You may have whatever you want," he said to Sa'id. "Shall it be silver and gold to buy a stall in the *suq?* Or do you want new clothing and a better job for your uncle?"

Sa'id stood straight and tall. "All I ask is that you annul your decree against my people. Let the Jews remain in their homes within the walls of San'a."

The king sent his chief adviser to bring the decree from the archives. When he returned, the king destroyed the document with his own hands. Then he said to the boy, "Now you have your wish. Go and live in peace."

Sa'id and Rabbi Salih returned home. The Jews of San'a had been spared, once again, and all gave thanks to God.

THE DREAMERS

◆   ◆   ◆

In Yemen, people believe dreams can foretell the future. They know the biblical story of how Joseph warned Pharaoh of Egypt about the meaning of his dreams and thereby saved the country from starvation. So Na'ama was not surprised when her husband, Yehya, a poor Yemenite Jew, awoke one morning and said, "I had a wonderful dream last night. I saw a ladder with a thousand steps and the king of Yemen upon it. I wish I knew the meaning of such a dream."

Na'ama did not know its meaning, either, but she advised her husband to go to the king and tell him the dream. "Since he is in your dream, perhaps he will understand it," she said.

At first Yehya hesitated. What if his dream angered the king? But then curiosity overcame fear, and Yehya hurried to the palace as fast as his sandaled feet would take him.

When at last he was admitted into the king's presence, he bowed and began, "My beloved king, last night I dreamed of a ladder with a thousand steps. It stretched between earth and heaven, and you were upon it. But when you had climbed halfway to the top, you stopped. Then I awoke."

To the poor Yemenite's great relief, the king smiled and thanked him for coming. Then he gave Yehya five hundred pieces of gold, one

for each step he had climbed in the dream. "Your dream portends a great future for me," said the king.

The news of Yehya's fortune spread quickly. Many friends came to touch the gold and hear the story of his visit to the king. Although good wishes overflowed the hearts of most of the visitors, the heart of Salame, the wife of Musa, held only envy. Later, when they had returned home, she told her husband, "I want you to dream something wonderful tonight. Then you will tell your dream to the king and be rewarded with even more gold."

Musa went right to bed and did his best to dream, but in the morning he could remember nothing. The next night he tried again, but his sleep was as peaceful as a baby's. Salame's scolding did no good. It just kept him awake. At last Salame said, "Since you cannot really dream, you'll just have to invent one for the king."

Obediently Musa tried with all his might to think of something as wonderful as a ladder that reached from earth to heaven, but he could not. Finally Salame said, "I shall have to invent a dream myself, and you shall tell it to the king."

Musa trembled at the thought of lying to his king, but he was more afraid of his wife and so agreed to her plan. Within a week Salame had invented a dream. She coached her husband. "Repeat my story exactly, and we shall be even richer than Yehya."

The words were easy to remember, and when Musa was in the presence of the king, he began to speak as he had been taught. He used some of Yehya's very words. "My beloved king, last night I dreamed of a ladder with a thousand steps. It stretched between earth and heaven, and you were climbing upon it. When you reached the very top, you stood there gazing down at your kingdom. Then I awoke."

This time the king did not smile. Instead he angrily ordered one thousand lashes to be given to Musa, one for each step of the ladder.

Musa quaked with fear. What had gone wrong? Surely he had repeated the lie exactly as he had learned it. "Oh, beloved king, I do not understand. My friend Yehya received five hundred pieces of gold when he told you of his dream, and I am to receive a thousand lashes!"

The king answered, "Your dream was an evil one. You should have kept it to yourself."

"But it was almost the same dream," Musa pleaded. "The same ladder stretching from earth to heaven. The same number of steps. What was wrong with my dream?"

"Yehya saw me halfway to the top with five hundred steps yet to ascend," replied the king. "Your dream had me already at the top, and I had nowhere to go—except down."

When the news of Musa's painful visit to the king reached Yehya and Na'ama, they decided not to approach the king with any more of their confusing dreams but to puzzle them out alone. After all, since no one could be sure of the future, their guess was as good as the king's—and far less risky, too.

MOSHE THE MISER

◆ ◆ ◆

Moshe lived in a small town in Yemen. Only a stranger would have asked Moshe for charity, as it was well known he never gave anything to anyone. He did, however, provide friendly greetings as he wished his fellow Jews, *"Mo'adim LaSimchoh"* on Rosh Hashanah and *"Sabboth Sholem"* on the Sabbath.

The Jews in this town, like Jews all over Yemen, willingly paid a tax that supported the poor, the sick, and the elderly. Yet Moshe the miser never contributed a single rial. The rabbi tried to reason with him. "Moshe, you cannot take your money with you."

"Without charity, the sick will have to get well and the poor will seek work," Moshe told the rabbi. "As for the elderly, they should have planned for their old age."

The years passed, and the rabbi never abandoned his efforts to get something from Moshe. He tried anger and public humiliation and even flattery. But nothing loosened the smallest coin from Moshe's leather purse. Then one day, without warning, the miser died.

There were few mourners at his funeral. The rabbi read the customary prayers, and Moshe was buried in a far corner of the cemetery. No stone was erected on his grave, and within a few weeks it was as if he had never lived.

Since the miser had no family, any money he left would go to the congregation. The rabbi and the elders of the community searched Moshe's house, but they found nothing more than a few coins in his leather purse. "Perhaps he did take his fortune with him," joked the *nassi,* the leader of the congregation. But the rabbi did not smile. He felt a stab of conscience as he remembered how he had tormented Moshe all those years.

Some time later, Tamara, a widow with six children, came in great excitement to see the rabbi. "Yesef the sandalmaker says if I don't settle my entire debt with him at once he will take me to court!" Tamara shook a piece of paper under the rabbi's nose. "But see . . . our agreement says I can pay a little each week. I think Yesef has gone crazy!"

At that very moment the wife of Harun the wood seller rushed in. Tears streamed down her face as she sobbed, "My husband has decided to become a beggar and make me into a beggar's wife. I think he has lost his mind!"

Before the rabbi could say a word of comfort, Salem the peddler appeared. Shaking with anger, he shouted, "I have been in business with Azri the basketmaker for twenty years. Now he has thrown me out. The man is mad!"

The rabbi did not know what to think. Yesef, Harun, and Azri had always been honest, industrious men. At last the rabbi found his voice. "Go home, my friends," he counseled. "Let me see what I can do."

The rabbi called first on Yesef. He found the sandalmaker sitting cross-legged on his mat, stitching a leather strap. "Why have you demanded full payment from Tamara after all this time?" the rabbi asked.

Yesef replied, "I have extended credit to Tamara and dozens of others for more years than I can remember. Although some pay a little every week, others do not. Only because I had a benefactor could I stay in business." Yesef shrugged his shoulders and concluded, "But things change. From now on I must depend on myself."

How surprised the rabbi was to learn that such a generous person lived in the community. A man like that should be thanked by the entire congregation. But when asked for the benefactor's name, Yesef would only say, "I have given my word never to reveal his identity." The rabbi pleaded with Yesef but to no avail. Yesef's word was his word.

At the house of the wood seller, the rabbi found Harun occupied in ripping his ragged shirt to make it look even worse. "Why are you becoming a beggar?" asked the rabbi. "You have always sold plenty of wood. In fact, you sold it more cheaply than anyone else. You even gave it away to the poor!"

"That was when I had a benefactor to support me," said Harun. "Now I have to take care of myself."

Naturally the rabbi wanted to know the name of Harun's benefactor. "Such a man has earned the community's gratitude," he said.

Harun shook his head, for he had made a solemn pledge never to tell. The rabbi pleaded, but Harun paid no more attention to his words than he did to the tears of his wife.

Finally the rabbi went to the shop of Azri. It was situated in the corner of the *suq* and piled high with baskets of every size and shape. "Why have you broken off your partnership with Salem?" the rabbi asked.

Azri threw back his head and laughed. His strong white teeth were like those of a lion. "For years I have given Salem the baskets I make that are less than perfect. He has paid me nothing and sells them for very little to the poor. I could afford to be generous, for I had a benefactor to support me. But now things are different. I shall have to sell those baskets myself."

When the rabbi asked for the benefactor's name, Azri refused to answer, saying, "I promised to keep his name a secret from the world."

Irritated now beyond tolerance, the rabbi returned to the synagogue. His duty was clear. Somehow, he had to learn the names of the three benefactors and honor them publicly.

A week later the rabbi held a meeting in the synagogue. Everybody was expected to attend, even the women, who were often excused from community concerns. The rabbi began, "Among us live three men whose generosity has benefited us all, in one way or another. I call upon Yesef, Harun, and Azri to remove the seal from their lips and name them."

No one said a word. There was not a whisper or a cough or even a sigh. Yesef, Harun, and Azri stared straight ahead, as if they had not heard. The rabbi stood directly in front of them and said, "I will now ask God to release you from your vows so that our congregation will be free from the sin of ingratitude."

All eyes were fixed on the rabbi as he began to sway in prayer. Every ear strained to hear his chanting. At last he said to the three men, "Your vows are no longer vows; your promises are no longer promises; your obligations are no longer obligations. For the sake of the congregation, you are free to speak."

Each man rose slowly to his feet and revealed the name of his benefactor. But instead of three different names, only one was uttered: Moshe the miser. His name echoed and reechoed in the minds and hearts of the congregation. The words beat against the windows and doors of the synagogue and flew outside and up to the ears of God.

The men and women whispered the name to themselves and recalled how disrespectfully the miser had been treated. The rabbi's own conscience pained him deeply. How he had bullied and shamed the man. And Moshe's funeral! How shabby it had been.

The rabbi stammered, "Why . . . did you not tell me about Moshe's good deeds after his death? We would have given him the kind of funeral he deserved."

Azri answered, "We tried to become *his* benefactors, for he believed in the rabbinic precept that says, 'Do not become famous through charity.'"

A short time later the entire congregation visited Moshe's neglected grave. The rabbi himself pulled out the overgrown grass and helped to place the tombstone. It read simply: MOSHE BEN NISSIM. . . "Now his name and the name of his father are linked to the living," the rabbi said. Then the rabbi asked God to forgive him and the Jewish community for their insensitive and judgmental ways.

As the years passed, the miser's grave became known as a holy place, and Jews from all over Yemen went there to pray. Perhaps they believed Moshe's good deeds would incline God's ear to them. Perhaps they believed by visiting a good person's grave, they would become better people. Their thoughts can only be guessed at, but one fact is clear: In death, Moshe the miser became more famous than he was in life—and for much better reasons.

THE NAGGING WIFE

◆ ◆ ◆

Sa'ada often quarreled with her husband, Mashulom. Day and night his ears rang with her complaints. "My clothes are shabby," she told him. "I have no jewelry, and our house is little more than a pile of stones."

Mashulom did the best he could. He wove baskets from early morning until daylight faded, but his work brought him little money. Even for Shabbat, Sa'ada could rarely afford to buy a chicken or a piece of meat. Barley, millet, and fresh vegetables were the usual daily fare.

One evening when Mashulom came home, he brought a present for Sa'ada. That day a rich customer had paid him handsomely for a basket. Although Mashulom had protested, the man insisted he accept an extra rial, exclaiming, "A fine basket is a fine basket!"

With this money Mashulom had bought a length of beautiful red cloth so Sa'ada could make herself a dress. But instead of dancing about with delight and measuring the cloth against herself as Mashulom had expected, his wife had flown into a rage. "Where would I go in a new dress? Besides, I have no shoes. I think you bought this to shame me!"

Mashulom protested that he had only wanted to please her, but Sa'ada would not listen. At last she stormed, "I have had enough of poverty with you. I am going to live with my mother!"

One might suppose Mashulom would breathe a sigh of relief at the prospect of living in peace and quiet, but he didn't. "Please stay with me, Sa'ada," he begged, "and you will have shoes and jewelry and whatever else your heart yearns for. I shall work even harder!"

But Sa'ada had made up her mind. The next morning she wrapped a loaf of newly baked bread in a cloth and set out for her mother's house.

Sa'ada had been to visit her mother only once since her marriage. On that journey of a day and a night, she had danced along the dusty road beside Mashulom. The sun scorched them, the night chilled them, but she did not notice. Married but a short time, she loved Mashulom with all her heart and wanted nothing more than his company.

Now all was different. The sun had never seemed so fierce, and when night came and the moon rose, shadows of a thousand terrors frightened her. Mile after mile she hurried, tormented by her imagination. She dared not rest, for fear an evil spirit might be waiting for her behind each rock or bush.

Suddenly a lion leapt from behind a huge boulder onto the road. His emerald eyes gleamed in the moonlight. His teeth glistened. Sa'ada walked more quickly. She prayed the lion would not notice her, but of course he did. He followed after her, and soon she felt his hot breath against her neck. Sa'ada began to run, but no matter how fast she raced, the lion kept pace. At every step she expected to be devoured.

Then Sa'ada remembered the bread she carried. Perhaps the lion would accept the loaf and forget all about eating her. She did bake delicious millet bread. Sa'ada pulled the bread free from the cloth and tossed it over her shoulder.

The lion didn't miss a step. He snatched up the bread in his powerful jaws and kept right on running. He stayed so close to Sa'ada that she could have touched him if she dared.

At last Sa'ada arrived at her mother's house. "Save me, Mother!" Sa'ada cried, trying to beat against the door with her fists. Her strength was almost gone, and her mother heard only a faint noise—as if the wind had murmured her name. Cautiously she opened the door, and Sa'ada fell into her arms. "A lion has been following me all night. He is about to eat me!" she cried, trembling with fear.

The green eyes of the lion flashed with anger. He dropped the bread and nipped Sa'ada on the leg.

The young woman screamed out in pain, and her mother helped her inside to lie down against soft pillows. She bandaged the shallow wound, then sang to Sa'ada until she fell asleep.

In the morning Sa'ada awoke to a breakfast of broth and fresh fruit. "How is it you have come without your husband?" her mother asked.

"I have left Mashulom," Sa'ada said. She explained what a poor provider he was and how unhappy he had made her.

Sa'ada's mother answered, "Foolish child. You complain that your clothes are shabby, but have you considered how fortunate you are to have your husband's respect? It dresses you as royally as any princess."

"But I have no gold necklaces or bracelets," Sa'ada grumbled.

"You have your husband's love," her mother pointed out. "Love makes a woman glow with beauty. She needs no other adornment."

Sa'ada pouted. "What about my house? It is a pile of stones."

"Your husband works hard, my daughter. It is his industry that shelters you."

The next morning Sa'ada and her mother went to draw water from the village well. Before they had gone more than a few steps, the mother stumbled against something in her path. Stooping down, she picked up the bread the lion had dropped. She recognized the loaf at once, for she herself had taught Sa'ada how to form a loaf in that special way.

She held out the bread for her daughter to examine. Not a tooth

mark dented the smooth, golden crust. "How gentle the lion was," exclaimed Sa'ada. "But why did he follow me if he meant no harm?"

"Perhaps God sent the lion to watch over you. Or the lion himself may have seen that such a foolish young woman needed protection."

Sa'ada felt a sudden rush of gratitude toward the lion. He *had* kept her from harm during that long and fearsome journey. And she felt a new awakening of love and gratitude toward her husband. Did Mashulom not work to keep her safe from hunger and nakedness and the terror of the world?

Then Sa'ada gave thanks to God. In spite of her sharp tongue and foolish ways, he had protected and preserved her.

"It is time for me to return home," Sa'ada said, and her mother agreed.

Sa'ada dusted off the bread, wrapped it in her cloth, and started off. This time the way did not seem so long nor so frightening. As soon as she entered her house she kissed Mashulom and began fashioning a dress from the red cloth he had brought her.

THE PURCHASE

◆　◆　◆

Once a Jewish trader by the name of Madhmun started for the *suq* in San'a to buy bulls. He had filled his purse with rials and looped two ropes over his shoulder to lead the bulls home. He prided himself on being a shrewd buyer and felt confident of striking a good bargain.

As he walked along the dusty road leading from his village to San'a, he saw an old man whose *zunner* marked him as a Jew. A slender, barefoot boy walked beside the old man. As Madhmun drew near, the old man called to him and asked, "Where are you going, my son?"

"I am going to buy some bulls," said Madhmun, respectful of the man's white beard and wrinkled cheeks. He tried to move on, but the man would not let him pass. "My son, why do you not add 'with the permission of God'?"

Madhmun laughed. "God has nothing to do with buying bulls," he answered, and went on his way.

When Madhmun arrived at the stall of the cattle merchant, he saw many fine bulls. Some pawed the ground, snorted a fine mist from their quivering nostrils, and rolled their eyes. Others stood still except for their switching tails. Madhmun took a long time to make up his mind. He wanted neither a dull animal nor one with too much spirit.

At last he chose two sturdy bulls with shiny coats and soft brown eyes. He offered a low price, much less than the bulls were worth. The merchant responded with a higher price, much higher than he could expect to receive. After much more discussion the price was set. Madhmun felt he had got the best of the merchant, and the merchant believed he had got the best of Madhmun.

Madhmun slipped the ropes he had brought over the heads of the bulls. Holding the ends of the ropes in one hand, he opened his leather purse with the other. To Madhmun's astonishment, the purse was empty! "I must have lost my money on the way," Madhmun explained to the merchant. "Please do not sell these bulls to anyone else. I shall return at once with the money."

Madhmun raced home to fill his purse again. This time he pulled the leather strap more tightly and tied it to his belt. Taking the same road, he hurried toward San'a again. But just before he reached the city, the old Jew and the young boy stopped him. "Where are you going this time, my son?" the old man asked.

Madhmun's impatience made him rude. "I told you before. I am going to buy some bulls. Let me pass."

"You should say 'with God's mercy,'" advised the old man.

"I only need money, not mercy," replied Madhmun, continuing quickly on his way.

The boy left the old Jew and ran after Madhmun. He followed him all the way to the *suq*, but Madhmun paid no attention. His mind was on the bulls. If only they had not been sold.

Luckily the bulls were still waiting for him. The ends of their ropes dangled in the dust. The cattle merchant had been waiting, too, and held out his hand for the money. Madhmun untied the strap and shook his leather purse over the outstretched hand of the merchant. But nothing fell out.

The merchant roared with anger. "You are trying to make a fool of me! I could have sold these bulls ten times over!"

Madhmun insisted he was an honest man and begged for one more chance. "I shall return before you are an hour older," he promised wildly, and, doubling his speed, raced back home.

The young boy ran after him again, but Madhmun did not care who followed him so long as he could get more money and buy his bulls. Half-dead with exhaustion, Madhmun filled his purse, shoved it inside his cotton *zinnah,* and again ran toward San'a. The boy kept pace with him although his breath did not come in such great gasps as did Madhmun's.

Just as they were about to enter San'a, Madhmun saw the old man again. "My son, what is so important that your face sweats as if the rain had poured down on it from heaven?" he cried.

"I . . . am . . . going . . . to . . . buy . . . some . . . bulls," Madhmun gasped as he raced on.

"You should say 'by God's mercy, blessed be God's name,'" the old man called after him.

But Madhmun did not answer. He had scarcely breath enough to reach the *suq.* The boy sped after him, matching him stride for stride.

Madhmun arrived at the cattle stall so tired he could scarcely stand. The merchant said hotly, "No more tricks now, or I will call the king's soldiers to arrest you!"

"I'm going . . . to . . . buy those . . . bulls," Madhmun managed to wheeze.

The boy looked up at him with sadness in his great dark eyes and shook his head. After a moment of recognition Madhmun added hoarsely, "With the permission and mercy of God, blessed be God's name."

Then Madhmun slowly pulled out his purse. It bulged with rials. Not only did it hold the bulls' purchase price, but it also held all the missing money Madhmun had put into it earlier.

Madhmun paid for the bulls and led them from the stall. Then he pressed a rial into the hand of the boy. "Take this, my friend, and ask the old man to forgive me."

Madhmun strode swiftly, his tiredness gone. He had completed his purchase, and now he would lead his splendid bulls home—with the permission and mercy of God, blessed be God's holy name.

THE WOODCUTTER

◆ ◆ ◆

Once a Jewish woodcutter came to the marketplace in San'a to sell a load of kindling. He had piled the sticks of wood high on the back of his faithful donkey, and as he guided the beast through the narrow, twisting streets, he called out a warning, "Make way! Make way!"

A group of idle young boys decided to have some fun with the woodcutter. Ali, their leader, hoped to frighten the donkey into either running away or spilling the kindling onto the street. Perhaps it would do both!

Suddenly Ali began to wave his arms and yell at the donkey. The animal, however, was too well trained to pay any attention. He simply plodded along next to his master, who kept calling, "Make way! Make way!"

Unwilling to give up so easily, Ali bent down to shout directly into the donkey's ear. A moment later he cried out in great pain. A piece of kindling had poked him in the eye. Ali's friends grabbed the woodcutter and his donkey and held them fast. "We'll teach you not to hurt people who are only trying to have a little fun," one of them threatened.

"Let's take him to the court," said Ali, cupping his hand over his injured eye. "The judge will punish him severely for blinding an

innocent boy who was walking along minding his own business!"

Greatly discouraged, the woodcutter went along to the court. He didn't expect to get a fair hearing. After all, what judge would believe a Jew's story—especially without someone to speak in his favor? The woodcutter patted the nose of his only witness and said sadly, "Loyal friend, if only you could tell them the truth."

At the court Ali and the others were so eager to convict the woodcutter that they all chattered at the same time. The judge held up his hand for silence and called on the injured boy to speak first. "Tell me exactly what happened to you," he said.

"My left eye is blind because of this Jew and his stupid donkey," Ali said. "The Jew had piled too much wood on his donkey. As I walked past, a stick of kindling slipped and poked me in the eye. He should have warned people to stay clear of the donkey, but he didn't open his mouth."

The judge turned to the woodcutter. "And what do you say to the boy's charge?" he asked.

The woodcutter did not reply. He looked as unconcerned as his donkey.

The judge explained the charge to the woodcutter again. "Now how do you answer? What is your defense?"

Still the woodcutter remained silent.

Annoyed, the judge tried a third time. "Listen to me, Jew. This young man says you are at fault for injuring his eye. If you don't tell me your side, I am going to sentence you to jail and make you pay a fine of one hundred rials!"

The woodcutter still did not answer. He was occupied in scratching his donkey's ears with a small piece of kindling.

At last the judge said to the boys, "I have to let the Jew go. It is obvious to me the man is a mute and cannot hear us. He didn't call out because he cannot speak. For that he is not responsible. It is Allah's will."

At that all the boys began to chatter again, and Ali cried out in anger, "Mute, you say? How can the woodcutter be mute? Less than an hour ago we all heard his voice. With my own ears I heard him shout 'Make way! Make way!'"

At once the Jew left off scratching his donkey's ears and came to life. "You see, my lord? He has just admitted I did warn him. Is it my fault he did not listen?"

"Indeed it is not," said the judge, and released the woodcutter on the spot.

As soon as the Jew regained the street, he gave thanks for God's abundant mercies. Then he kissed the nose of his clever donkey and continued to the *suq* to sell his kindling.

YA'ISH AND THE PROTECTOR

◆ ◆ ◆

O ne year a terrible drought came to Yemen, and the king
issued two decrees. The first commanded all the Jews to
move beyond the protective walls of San'a and live in the
desert. But the second decree held out some hope: it declared if the
prayers of the Jews brought rain, the first decree would be annulled.

Naturally the Jews prayed with all their heart and soul for rain. The
rabbi even directed the congregation to carry the Torah to the
cemetery and pray there so as to catch God's attention more quickly.
But still the heavens remained shut, and no rain fell.

At last the Jews held a lottery in the synagogue. They chose a man
named Ya'ish to travel to the land of the sons of Moses, where the ten
lost tribes dwelt, and ask for help. This land was situated very far away,
on the other side of the dangerous River Sambatiyon. During the week
the current was strong and swift. On the Sabbath the river rested, but
its waters were covered by searing flames. With such protection no
thoughtless traveler could disturb the Sabbath peace of the sons of
Moses.

The rabbi said to Ya'ish, "Swim the river just before the Sabbath
begins, as the current will be less swift and the flames won't have had
time to spread. Explain to the sons of Moses that if we are forced to
move from the protection of the city walls, we shall be easy prey

for the bandits that roam the desert looking for people to rob and kill.''

Since Ya'ish had no wife or family to provide for, he left at once and walked for many days until he reached the River Sambatiyon. He arrived just as the sun was beginning to set. It was almost time for another Sabbath to begin. The current was slowing, and in a few moments the river would burst into flames. Quickly Ya'ish dove into the water and swam with all his might to the other side.

As he pulled himself up on the bank he saw a woman hurrying along, balancing a jar of water on her head. She had just come from the well and had to be home before the Sabbath began. Ya'ish called to her softly, for he did not want to startle her. The woman did not hear but continued to walk rapidly. Fearing she might walk right out of his sight and seeing no one else to ask for directions, Ya'ish tossed a pebble at her jar. It chipped the rim, and a few drops of water spilled.

The woman stopped and looked around. She became frightened at seeing a stranger with mud-streaked clothing, but Ya'ish smiled and said gently, ''Do not be afraid. Can you tell me where I can find the sons of Moses?'' The woman did not answer but made a sign for him to follow her. On reaching her house, she rushed inside to set down the jar of water. Then she motioned to Ya'ish to follow her again. It was almost dark when they arrived at the synagogue. She left him and went to the women's section to pray.

Ya'ish joined the men and chanted the familiar prayers. He might have been in his own synagogue in San'a. At the end of the service he was given food and a place to rest but not a word of conversation. He spent the next day at the synagogue, saying his Sabbath prayers, but still no one spoke to him.

After the havdalah service signaling the end of the Sabbath, the people did speak. They gathered around Ya'ish and accused him of

traveling on their holy day of rest. "You entered the synagogue after the service had begun," said the *nassi*, the leader of the congregation. "You have been traveling for a long time and have no respect for our Sabbath."

Ya'ish did his best to argue against their charges, but no one would listen to him. Not until the woman stepped forward to show the chipped place on her jar did they believe him. And not until she told how considerate and polite Ya'ish was in asking for directions did they agree to hear why he had come to seek them out.

Ya'ish explained the plight of the Jews in San'a and asked for their help in ending the drought. "Without rain we are doomed," he told them.

After a great deal of discussion the people agreed on a plan for San'a. They gave Ya'ish a scroll to be read in the synagogue. It held special prayers for rain. "And we are sending someone with you to protect the Jewish community—just in case the king fails to keep his word," the *nassi* said.

After another day's rest Ya'ish left for home. He was accompanied by a slender, smooth-faced, ordinary-looking fellow who was dressed simply except for a curious hat that completely covered his hair. He did not speak to Ya'ish and always stayed a few paces behind him.

After many days the weary travelers arrived in San'a and immediately entered the synagogue. The congregation had been waiting impatiently. They crowded about the rabbi as he gently removed the scroll from Ya'ish's arms. After unrolling it carefully, the rabbi began to read the prayers aloud in his strong, clear voice. As his words rang out a gentle rain began to fall. It fell night and day, day and night, until all the wells, springs, and rivers were full. Then the rain stopped.

How the Jews of San'a rejoiced! How pleased they were with Ya'ish. He was so brave, so clever! They treated the stranger politely but thought to themselves he wasn't needed. After all, the king had promised to annul his evil decree as soon as the drought was over. And now it was over!

But the king was like the Egyptian pharaoh who made promises to Moses long ago. He changed his mind. The king said to the Jews, "As it is a well-known law that Jews are forbidden to own weapons, it is obvious to me that you are unable to protect yourselves even within our walls. Therefore, it should make little difference to you whether you live in San'a or outside in the desert. Besides," he went on, "the population of San'a is growing, and my people need your houses."

Ya'ish, who had become the spokesman for the Jews since his triumphant return, replied that they were indeed able to defend themselves against San'a's multitudes since a protector now lived among them. Pointing to the man with the curious hat, Ya'ish said, "He can defend us against anyone who tries to do us harm."

The king quickly challenged the protector to a contest. "I will change my decree if your protector wins," the king declared. "But if he loses, then you must leave your homes at once."

On the following day many of the Jews walked to the king's palace to witness the contest. The king himself plucked a hair from the tail of a black horse and suspended it from a tree branch. The most skilled archer in the king's army shot at the hair, but the arrow missed. Calmly the protector stepped forward, took aim, and let the arrow fly. It snapped the hair in half.

With a respectful bow to the king the protector said, "Oh, gracious king, I have won. Now annul your decree and let the Jews live in peace."

But the king refused, saying a gnat had flown into the archer's eye, and challenged the protector to a second contest. This time both men would shoot at a target from the backs of racing camels.

The protector agreed, and the target was lashed to a tree. The men mounted the camels and urged them across the desert sands. Suddenly they wheeled about and raced toward the target. Again the arrows flew, and again the stranger from the land of the sons of Moses was the winner.

"Now, most noble king, let my people live in safety within the walls of San'a," entreated the protector.

But the king was sure a shaft of sunlight had blinded the archer just as he had released the arrow. Another contest was requested. "This time I will match my eldest son against you," the king said to the protector. "Each of you will have a chance to kill the other with a single blow. Do you accept?"

The protector hesitated, for this challenge was the most serious of all. Then he said, "I accept, beloved king, but first you must give me your word in writing to annul the decree against the Jews if I slay your son."

The king did not hesitate at all. His son was an expert swordsman and would prove more than a match for the puny youth with the funny hat. The king's scribe quickly wrote up the agreement, and the king signed it at once.

The contestants drew lots, and the king's tall, handsome son won the right to strike the first blow. He raised his sword high over the head of the protector and brought it down with lightning swiftness. The stranger, however, stepped deftly aside, and the sword whistled as it sliced the empty air.

Then the protector raised his sword against the king's son. "I am truly sorry to do this, great king, for your son is brave and strong. Yet I have heard your words and know this is your will."

Suddenly the king cried out, "Have mercy. Do not kill my son!"

The protector hesitated. With his arm still uplifted, he asked, "Noble king, will you promise to let my people live in peace within San'a's walls even if droughts again plague this land?"

"I give you my word," the king promised. And the protector put down his sword.

Then the king said to the protector, "I am curious about you. Why have you no beard like other Jews? And why do you wear such an odd hat?"

The protector answered softly, "Mighty king, the laws of my body do not permit me to grow a beard. And the laws of my people will not allow me to show my hair to others. My lord, I am a woman."

Ya'ish was too surprised to speak. How could it be that a woman had rescued the Jews of San'a from the king's evil decrees?

The king was surprised, too, but this time he kept his word. Even after the protector returned to the land beyond the River Sambatiyon, the king made sure that no harm befell the Jews and that they lived in peace thereafter.

ELIJAH'S MERCY

◆ ◆ ◆

In San'a there once lived a rich but miserly Jew who refused to give tzedakah to anyone. The poor who came to beg for a few coins or a little bread had been turned away from his door so many times, they had stopped coming. And, since the miser never went into the streets to seek out those who were in need, he had few opportunities to perform a mitzvah. Not that he cared, of course. He had no wish to help anyone in any way.

The angels in heaven wept in pity when they looked down upon the poor. "If only that miser would share a small part of his wealth, he could relieve so much suffering," they said. But as the years passed and the miser continued in his selfish ways, the angels grew impatient. They declared, "Such a wicked man does not deserve to live an hour longer in God's beautiful world," and they decreed that the miser must die.

But there was one person in heaven who asked for mercy. Elijah said to the angels, "Will you give him a little more time to change his ways?"

"We have waited for many years already," the angels replied, "but we will wait thirty days more. If at the end of that time he has become a charitable person, he will live. If not, he must die at once."

Elijah went immediately to the world below. He dressed himself in rags and appeared at the miser's house during the evening meal. The fragrance of food cooking drifted through the door when the miser opened it.

"I have heard you are a wealthy man," Elijah said with great humility. "I am dying of hunger. Will you give me a piece of bread so I may have the strength to look for work?"

"I have no bread to spare," answered the miser, and he shut the door in Elijah's face.

The next afternoon Elijah returned to the miser's house. The day was hot, and he found the wealthy man in his garden among the shady trees and splashing fountains. Elijah leaned weakly against a tamarind tree and said in a cracked voice, "Please, my lord, give me a sip of water. The sun has burned my skin, and my throat is as dry as the desert sands."

"I scarcely have enough water for my own household," replied the miser, and he drove Elijah from the garden.

On the third day the miser locked himself in his room to count his money, and Elijah appeared before him again. He was even shabbier than before. He was coughing and seemed in great pain as he said, "I am sick. Please give me a little money to buy medicine."

The miser thrust Elijah from his house, saying, "I don't know how you got in here, but go away and stop bothering me. I have only enough money to support my own family."

A few days later Elijah found the miser in his bath. He had left his clothes in a heap and was relaxing in the warm water with his eyes closed. Elijah quickly dressed himself in the miser's clothes and assumed the miser's face and manner. In fact, he was as much like the miser as the miser himself. When the servants saw him leaving the bath, they thought he was the head of the household.

Elijah entered the *diwan* to dine with the miser's wife and son. They did not notice anything different about the man who sat with them,

and they greeted him in the usual way. Just as the family began to eat, the miser himself ran naked into the room.

On seeing Elijah dressed in his very own robe, the miser began to scream, "Thief! Give me back my clothes!" Elijah told the wife and son to pay no attention to the man, adding, "He must be a crazy person." Then Elijah called the servants and told them to throw the wretch into the street.

"My clothes! My clothes!" babbled the miser.

But Elijah answered with the miser's own words, "I do not give away clothes. I have only enough for myself."

"But the poor man is naked," said the tenderhearted wife, who was close to tears. Elijah shrugged and said, "I noticed a pile of rags in the bath. Let him wear those."

So the miser dressed himself in Elijah's old clothes and had to go from house to house begging for food. His rags offered little protection from the fiery sun or the cold winds of night. He was so dirty and shabby, he could barely recall his earlier life of luxury and pleasure.

One hot afternoon he crept into the garden that used to be his. He hoped to shelter himself against the burning rays of the sun. Elijah, still dressed in the miser's clothes, found the ragged man standing in one of the fountains. He was trying to soothe his sore, aching feet in the cool water.

As soon as the miser saw Elijah, he jumped from the fountain and bowed before him. "My lord, I do not understand how it is you have become me and I have become you."

Elijah answered, "Let me tell you a story. Not long ago a poor man came to you and asked for a piece of bread. The next day he begged for a drink of water. The third time he pleaded for a few coins to buy medicine. Do you remember that wretched man?"

The miser nodded. "I remember—and I sent him away empty-handed. But what does that unfortunate fellow have to do with you?"

"I am Elijah, and I was that wretch. I gave you three chances to do a mitzvah and save your life. But you didn't take them. And now you have run out of time. Heaven has seen your wickedness and has condemned you to death."

On hearing those words, the miser almost fainted from fright. Miserable as his life was, it was still precious to him. "Is there nothing I can do to save my life?" the miser whimpered.

"You can lengthen your days by becoming charitable," answered Elijah. "Be merciful to others, and heaven will be merciful to you."

Suddenly the miser found himself alone. Elijah was gone, and his own clothes lay under a tree. He dressed quickly and ran to a nearby pond to see if he was truly himself again.

With great relief the miser saw his own familiar face in the wavy waters of the pond. Truly he was himself again, but at the same time he was different.

The rich man never knew if he had dreamed of Elijah or not, and in time Elijah's face faded from his mind. But his memories of hunger and suffering endured. Tzedakah became the rich man's way of life. Not only did he aid all those who arrived at his door in need of food, clothing, or shelter, but he also went into the streets each day to help the poor.

For the rest of the rich man's long, long life, he was known for his good deeds, and the angels in heaven rejoiced.

THE THREE WISE ACTS

◆ ◆ ◆

Once an elderly Jewish silversmith went by ship to Ethiopia and delivered a pair of magnificent candlesticks to a valued customer. But before he could return home the silversmith became ill. Sensing he would soon die, he summoned Abdallah, his customer, and pressed a leather bag of coins into his hand. "Will you keep this money for my son, Mas'ud? He will come for it when he hears I have died."

Abdallah hesitated, for he had never met Mas'ud. "Suppose someone else comes and pretends to be your son," Abdallah said. "How shall I know the truth?"

"By his deeds," answered the silversmith. "He will perform three wise acts."

"But what if he never arrives?"

"Then you may keep the money," the silversmith answered. Then he turned his face to the wall and died.

When the news of the father's death finally reached San'a, his family sat shivah and grieved. After the thirty days of mourning had passed, Mas'ud's mother said to him, "Go to Ethiopia, search for Abdallah, and return with the candlesticks or the money he paid to your father."

Obediently Mas'ud did as she asked. He booked passage on a ship

and sailed across the Red Sea. After landing he made his way to the small town where Abdallah lived. There, though he asked everyone he met for directions to Abdallah's house, no one would tell him. In that place all strangers were viewed with suspicion.

At last Mas'ud thought of a plan. After buying a bundle of kindling from a wood seller, he gave him an extra coin and said, "Deliver this to the house of Abdallah, for I wish to surprise him."

The wood seller was so pleased to be part of the secret that he took Mas'ud along the shortest route to Abdallah's fine house. Mas'ud knocked on the door, and when Abdallah opened it, Mas'ud said, "Here is the wood you ordered."

"I ordered nothing," Abdallah said.

Mas'ud smiled. "I know. I bought the kindling so I could follow the wood seller to your house. No one in your town would direct me here. I am Mas'ud, and I have come for the candlesticks or for the money you owed my father."

Abdallah invited Mas'ud inside, saying to himself, "That was clever, all right. He may be who he says, but I must test him further. Three wise acts, his father said."

As it was almost time for the noonday meal, Mas'ud accepted an invitation to eat and went to wash his hands. Abdallah whispered to his wife, "Cook five chickens, and we will see if this boy is wise enough to apportion them equally among seven people."

When they sat down to eat, Mas'ud was reluctant to apportion the chickens as Abdallah requested. That privilege belonged to the host. But at last Mas'ud consented. He gave one chicken to the husband and wife, one to the sons, one to the daughters, and kept two for himself.

Everyone finished quickly except Mas'ud. His two chickens took a long time to eat. At the end of the meal Mas'ud again said respectfully, "Please give me what is rightfully mine."

"In a while," said Abdallah, putting him off once more. "Spend the day with us, and we will speak of business later."

All afternoon Abdallah tried to decide if the young man had performed a second wise act or just didn't know how to count. Abdallah's wife didn't understand how Mas'ud had divided the chickens, either, but she had a plan. "Let me cook one chicken for our evening meal and see how he apportions *that*," she suggested to her husband.

Abdallah liked the idea and later, as they sat down to eat again, he asked Mas'ud to apportion the chicken fairly. Mas'ud tried to protest, but finally he agreed. This time he passed the head of the chicken to Abdallah, the heart to the wife, the wings to the daughters, the legs to the sons, and kept the entire body for himself.

This meal took Abdallah and his family even less time to eat. At the end, while they sat and watched Mas'ud finish his meal, Abdallah's wife whispered to her husband, "Whoever he is, he is clever enough to eat our food while we starve right in front of his eyes!"

At last Mas'ud was through eating. He thanked Abdallah for his hospitality and again asked for the money or the candlesticks.

Abdallah said, "First I must ask you something. Why did you apportion the chickens as you did at our midday meal?"

Mas'ud replied, "The servings had to be equal. You and your wife and one chicken made three. Your two daughters and a chicken were three. Your sons and a chicken were three. I took two chickens so we would also equal three."

"That was clever," murmured Abdallah's wife into her husband's ear. And he whispered back, "That's two."

"But tell me one thing more," Abdallah went on. "Why did you eat almost all of the chicken tonight? There was no equality in our starving and your feasting."

"You are the master of the house and worthy of the head," Mas'ud answered. "Your wife deserved the heart, for she is the most vital part of your household. The wings went to your daughters, who will soon be grown and fly away to husbands and houses of their own. As your sons are the pillars of your house and support it, I gave them the legs."

"And why did you take the body?" persisted Abdallah.

"Because it is shaped like a boat. I came in a boat as did my father, and I will leave in one. Now will you do as I ask?"

"With pleasure, for you have proved your identity beyond a doubt," answered Abdallah, and gave him his father's money.

Glossary of Yemenite Words and Phrases

Allah (<u>Ah</u>-lah)
Muslim name for God.

Bab-alroom (bahb-ahl-<u>room</u>)
Gate of the Jewish Quarter in San'a. (Ar.)

Diwan (dih-<u>wahn</u>)
Open court above ground level in a Jewish home in Yemen. (Ar.)

Havdalah (hahv-<u>duh</u>-luh)
Prayer service said at the conclusion of the Sabbath. (Heb.)

Hodeida (Hoh-<u>day</u>-duh)
Port in Yemen on the Red Sea.

Imam (ee-<u>mahm</u>)
An Arab religious/political leader. (Ar.)

Jambiyya (jahm-<u>bee</u>-yuh)
Razor-sharp, curved knife worn by Arabs. (Ar.)

Kiffiyya (kif-<u>fee</u>-yah)
Cloth headgear worn by Arabs. (Ar.)

Mitzvah (mitts-<u>vah</u>)
Good deed. (Heb.)

Mo'adim LaSimchoh (Moh-ah-<u>deem</u> Lah-seem-<u>kho</u>)
Greeting exchanged between Jews on Jewish holy days. (Heb.)

Nassi (nah-<u>see</u>)
Leader of a Jewish congregation. (Heb.)

Pita (<u>peet</u>-uh)
Flat bread with or without a pocket in the middle. (Ar.)

Qat (kat)
Mildly narcotic leaf chewed by Arabs. (Ar.)

Ramadan (Ra-mah-<u>dhan</u>)
The Islamic month of fasting.

Rial (ree-<u>ahl</u>)
Yemenite coin. (Ar.)

Rosh Hashanah (Rowsh-ha-Shah-<u>na</u>)
First day of the Jewish New Year. (Heb.)

63

Shabboth Sholem (Shah-<u>boht</u> Sho-<u>lehm</u>)	Greetings exchanged between Yemenite Jews on the Sabbath. (Heb.)
Shabbat (Shah-<u>baht</u>)	Sabbath. (Heb.)
Sambatiyon (Sahm-baht-<u>yohn</u>)	Mythical river.
San'a (<u>sah</u>-nah)	Capital city of Yemen.
Shivah (shih-<u>vah</u>)	Seven days of mourning. (Heb.)
Sirwal (sir-<u>wahl</u>)	Simple work pants worn by men. (Ar.)
Suq (suek)	Marketplace. (Ar.)
Talmud (<u>tahl</u>-muhd)	Book of Jewish laws and their commentaries. (Heb.)
Torah (toh-<u>rah</u>)	First five books of the Bible always hand-printed on parchment. (Heb.)
Tzedakah (tseh-dah-<u>kah</u>)	Charity. (Heb.)
Wadi (<u>wah</u>-dee)	Dry riverbed. (Ar.)
Yemen (<u>yeh</u>-men)	A country on the southwest of the Arabian Peninsula. It is now divided into the countries of North and South Yemen.
Zinnah (<u>zee</u>-nah)	Cloth belt. (Ar.)
Zunner (<u>zoo</u>-nahr)	Yellow turban Muslim law compelled Jews to wear. (Ar.)

Explanations:

Ar.	Arabic
Heb.	Hebrew

A Pronunciation Guide
to Yemenite names

Abdallah	Ahb-<u>dah</u>-lah	Ovediah	Oh-vuh-<u>dye</u>-uh
Ali	Ah-<u>lee</u>	Sa'ada	<u>Sah</u>-dah
Awad	Ah-<u>wad</u>	Sa'id	Sah-<u>eed</u>
Azri	<u>Ahz</u>-ree	Salame	Sah-<u>lah</u>-may
Elijah	Ee-<u>ly</u>-djuh	Salem	<u>Sah</u>-lehm
Harun	<u>Hah</u>-roon	Salih	<u>Sah</u>-leeh
Mashulom	Ma-<u>shoo</u>-lom	Salim	Sah-<u>leem</u>
Madhmun	Mahd-<u>muhn</u>	Tamara	Tah-<u>mah</u>-rah
Mas'ud	Mahs-<u>ood</u>	Ya'ish	Yah-<u>ish</u>
Moshe	Moe-<u>sheh</u>	Yehiel	Yeh-<u>hee</u>-el
Musa	<u>Moo</u>-sah	Yesef	<u>Yeh</u>-sef
Na'ama	<u>Nah</u>-ah-mah	Yehya	<u>Yeh</u>-yah
Nissim	Niss-<u>seem</u>		